The Happy Goat

by John Kershaw

with illustrations by
Gwen Green

Odhams Books
London · New York · Sydney · Toronto

One night there was a lot of excitement on the farm. A cow, a pig, a duck, a chicken, a sheep and a cat were standing in a circle in the barn, all talking at once.

On the ground in the middle of the circle lay a baby goat; a kid. It was lost and shy and frightened.

The old cat licked the goat's face and said, 'Miaow'. 'Miaow,' said the kid – which was very funny because goats should say, 'Bleat' not 'Miaow'.

The cat grinned and then introduced the kid to everyone. The cow chewed thoughtfully and said, 'Moo'. The pig grunted seriously and said, 'Snort'. The duck waddled about importantly and said, 'Quack'.

The chicken twitched her neck and said,
'Cluck'. And the sheep, who was nearly as
shy as the little goat, shook her wool straight
and said, 'Baa', very gently.

After that the other animals said goodnight
and went off to bed, while the little kid settled
down for his first night's sleep on the farm.

Early next morning the kid went out for a walk. He saw the cow in the milking-shed. 'Bleat,' he said. 'Moo,' said the cow, waving her tail. Then he saw the pig trotting into his sty. 'Bleat,' said the kid. 'Snort,' said the pig, most politely.

The duck crossed the farmyard to the muddy pond. 'Bleat,' called the kid. 'Quack,' shouted the duck. And the chicken said, 'Cluck', quite loudly, as the kid passed the henhouse.

He went back to the barn for his breakfast. The cat was in there lapping up a bowl of milk. 'Bleat,' said the kid. 'Miaow,' said the cat, shaking a drop of milk off her whiskers.

The kid felt much better this morning. He had looked around the farm and met the other animals again. And now he had a pile of fresh hay to eat and a bucket of water to drink.

When he'd finished, the little goat stood at the barn door, watching the farmer and the animals coming and going. And he began to

sing to himself. The tune was the same as, 'Baa, baa, black sheep'. But he didn't know that, of course.

He sang, 'Moo, snort, quack, cluck, baa, bleat, miaow. Moo, snort, quack, cluck, baa, bleat, miaow.' And, if you looked closely, you could almost see a smile on his face. After all, he was a happy little goat, now.